THE
SINNER

KURIEOUS WILLIAMS

WRITERS REPUBLIC L.L.C.
515 Summit Ave. Unit R1
Union City, NJ 07087, USA

Website: *www.writersrepublic.com*
Hotline: *1-877-656-6838*
Email: *info@writersrepublic.com*

Ordering Information:
Quantity sales. Special discounts are available on quantity purchases by corporations, associations, and others. For details, contact the publisher at the address above.

Library of Congress Control Number:		2019956876
ISBN-13:	978-1-64620-158-7	[Paperback Edition]
	978-1-64620-159-4	[Digital Edition]

Rev. date: 01/08/2020

CHAPTER 1

Thy Shall Not Commit Adultery

Are you committing adultery if you're not married but the other person is? Are you as guilty as them because you kept the act of adultery going? Temptation is a bitch! It's hard to fight especially when you're lonely and looking for attention. Some of us are weak, and I can attest to that. I am some of us! I am that sinner!

He was made for me but meant for someone else. We had been sneaking around for almost half of a year. What was casual for him was so much more to me. I began to fall in love with someone else's forever. It didn't bother me because I wasn't thinking rationally nor logically about the situation. Emotions got the best of me, and I couldn't see clearly. He was perfect in my eyes, well, minus the cheating; but I felt our souls connected every time he kissed me. But still it was wrong. Wrong of him to cheat on a woman who adored him, the woman who built her fairy tale with him. It was wrong of me because the fairy tale she had was the same fairy tale I wanted to have and was searching to build with someone.

It bothered me a lot to know that after every time we had sex, he left me alone. So one day I looked her up online to see why her and not me. What was it about this woman that made him stay? Once I found her online, that was when it hit me. The look in her eyes as she is embraced by her king and the look in his eyes to have such a strong queen standing beside him. How could I allow half of a year to go by and I'm spreading my legs to this man? Not to mention we weren't even using protection and I was not on any birth control plan as I lied to him. I was dazzled by those pretty brown eyes, sweet smile, confident conversation, gentle hugs, and the motivation he gave a broken girl. Still he wasn't mine, right? What I was doing was tearing another woman apart! I tried to justify in my head that I wasn't wrong, but indeed I was. Although he was married and I wasn't, I should have said no. If it wasn't me, it would have been someone else. One thing that puzzled my mind was all those late-night visits and sneaking around at our job; She had to know something wasn't right, or did they have one of those open relationships that I hear about? Which leads me to my next affair!

They were together for years and had a blended family. I came along in the midst of the breakup. I was just a two-year temporary girlfriend until they repaired what was broken in their relationship. I became a wonderful stepmom to a handsome young fellow although there were two kids. The beautiful little girl belonged to someone else. I figured he was still messing around when he and I were together. It was okay because I was also messing around with a few men and even one of his close friends (although he was in a relationship, but anyways we'll talk about that later). I met him through his best friend. The best friend I stated I had relations with. He and I began casual dating, and then I moved into his mom's house with him. Around this time I was unemployed and just got out of a same-sex relationship and moved back home. Things were rough when I moved back home, so I was looking for a way to escape. I ran into the best friend and together we plotted. We'll call the best friend Alex. Alex was in a relationship, and he wanted me too. The plot Alex came up with is, I mess with his best friend but don't get to serious and I still get to sleep with him. Anyways, as the guy and I started dating, I completely ignored Alex's plot and indeed got serious with the dude. We became inseparable, and for once I felt love for a man. We eventually moved out his mom's house and into our own spot. Him, his son, and myself—a family of my own. Things started to get rough, and I became the breadwinner and he the stay-at-home dad. (The shoe had switched foot.) He was an amazing provider when he was still working, and when I was working, I had forgotten how good he was to me.

I slept with many people and continue to sleep with Alex. He and I argued a lot, but the sex was so amazing that eventually I didn't mind sharing it. I'll never forget the moment we separated, the look he had in his eyes and the coldness I had in mine. I shut the door right in his face and went right back to sleep. (Yes, his bags were on the porch and his son was in his arms.) Over the years we would mess around even though he and his child's mother were back together. Eventually, his baby mother would watch us having sex, and then she too would join us. (I had a boyfriend, and we were living together. Yes, Alex was still around.)

I'll never forget this moment though, perhaps the last moment of our threesome fetish. I had just moved into my new place and the baby mama texted me and wanted to hang out. I already knew what time it was, so I texted him and basically said they could come over. We drank, smoked, played cards, and dared each other. She had just won, so she dared him to fuck me for a minute. At that minute, her facial expression changed and killed my mood. Her eyes looked hurt and deceived. I knew she could tell he was still in love with me and that I turned him on more than her. Her body gestures were in complete disbelief, and all I could think about is, *Damn, what have I done, and why couldn't I just resist this damn temptation?* No woman deserves this although she thinks that'll keep him. Then, again, some people like threesome activities. Which leads me to my next affair.

She and I had met through our best friends. (My best friend and her best friend were related.) She was so beautiful and exotic to me that I couldn't resist her. We would flirt, which eventually led us to having sex. We had lost contact but eventually found one another through her new profound love. She had had a beautiful baby with this crazy guy, who I would eventually have a threesome with. Eventually, our love affair would be a secret, behind her child's father back, until one day when we all had drinks and things escalated. What was a one-time thing became occasionally, even with other men at times. Soon we lost contact over her jealous child's father. But like always we would eventually get back into contact and the love affair would pick back up, until she moved miles away with another woman. I was hurt because I could have gone with her, but I stayed behind. When she came back closer to me, she was living with a new man. Remember we're close friends and sometimes much more. I met her new dude once she moved back, and he seemed cool. He thought I was just a friend, but he didn't know the dirty secrets we shared. I ate at their dinner table, and when he wasn't watching, I was eating her and she was eating me in the bed they shared while he went to work. She was now into a polygamist lifestyle, and I was down for it but not the commitment part. Eventually, I would have a threesome with her and her new beau. But then I pulled away because I wasn't into him. I guess I wasn't into him because I knew he was good to her and I didn't want to be the reason that would lead them to a breakup. Which leads me to my next affair. (I could go on about our secrets, but that's another story.)

I met him while getting back on my feet. He had asked for my number as I was working but it wasn't months until we actually hung out. I gave him a shot because he was persistent and I finally was on my feet, good enough where I didn't have to whore around and could focus on one person. He would be my downfall and the reason it took a long time to get back on my feet. We began to date, and eventually, I moved out of my own spot just to live with him. Our sex was intense until the point he ripped my vagina and I ended in the emergency room. While being examined, I found I had an infection that antibiotics could clear up. I was so afraid that he or someone else might have given me something. Once I questioned him, he told me he has herpes in his mouth (HSV-1 or oral herpes). Luckily, I wasn't exposed to that and I continued to sleep with him but took precautions. He and I began to get real serious, and I had actually found someone I was willing to commit to. He had a secret though, which I eventually found out through a late-night text. He had many infidelities, but this one right here made me pack my bags and leave. (Karma had finally came knocking at my door, and like a fool, I answered!) She had called one night while he was sleep, so being the curious person that I am, I answered. We began to talk, and she told me things about me that he had been saying to her. Apparently, she was the girlfriend and I was a friend who he was helping out. All those nights he would leave me in bed, claiming to be at his best friend's house or at work, he was with her. I wasn't mad at him nor her. I was mad at myself. I was so pissed off at myself because I had become the old me, messing around with another woman's man. I was so stupid I was willing to work it out with this guy and even be his side woman. I didn't care as usual that he had already built something with another woman; I just didn't want to feel that loneliness again. After we separated, we continued to sleep around. I was weak and didn't know how to be strong. I always went back to the past, which led me to my next affair.

I met him when I was eighteen. We were a secret because he's was old enough to be my dad and he was a family friend. I stop messing around with him about five years, and when I came back around, he had a baby who he claimed was supposed to have been mine. I left again, which lasted five more years; and this time, when I came back, he was married. That still didn't stop him from trying to get to me and that didn't stop me from fighting temptation. Once again I was with a married man and a man who has a new family.

See, this was how it happened. Soon as I turned eighteen, he was there. My life had been a struggle, and I had to make ends meet by any means necessary. He would sneak into my house, and we would have sex. For a time I actually liked him, but then my greed took advantage of his kindness. He supplied me with money to support my family, so in return I would supply him with a good time. Every weekend we would get away and I would bring a friend. We would party so hard and just have a good ole time from drinking to stripping. I would ask my friend to watch us as we have sex, and if she wanted to join, she could. Sometimes I would get him to leave just so I could have some fun with my friend or I would take his car and go visit a guy I was into. I never understood why this man was so in love with me. I would take off with his money and promised him a bunch of bullshit (still he always came back). I've cursed him out numerous time, but still, I can call him right now and he'll come and see me. I'm not going to lie that the fact he got married still bothered me. Within ten years of knowing him he had a baby and got married while I was still out there destroying families and marriages. Which leads me to my final affair.

He made it very clear that he was happy, but I couldn't help but wonder why he was stepping outside his marriage. We would occasionally meet, and he would gift me with things I need and not wanted. See, I was in a bad place at the time and struggling. For years we would creep around, and he would financially help me out. He never gave me the money but put it directly where it needed to go. Some days we would talk for hours, and he would just leave. He enlightened me on life, but it wasn't registering with me because as it went in one ear then it came out the other. I would counsel him on his relationship and advise him to be with her. He never visited at night, always in the daytime, and we would always meet in the same hotel room. From the way he made love to me, I could tell he was falling for me, so I start distancing myself, and eventually, the affair was done. Occasionally, he would inbox me and want to rekindle the fling we had, but I would always decline.

We were coworkers, and we would meet early before our shift to get a quickie. He had a wife and kids, and she would eventually find out about the affair. He would let me escape with goodies and always made sure I had enough. He was such a sweet guy and so kind to me. I could always get over on him, and he would still be waiting at my door. I had two other guys that would visit me at this job, and it would bother him, but I didn't care. There was nothing sexual with them, though they enjoyed my conversation and always pursued me. One of them was married and the other was dating. Eventually, that job ended and so did the attention I gave to all three guys.

See, he was never mine and I was never his. He was separated from his wife, and I was lonely. We linked up on some sexual activities, which led us to living together. We began to build together and plan a future. (But how can you build with someone who already has a future with someone?) He and his wife were separated and planned on getting a divorce (well, that's what I was told). She had a restraining order out on him, and I just assumed that it was because he was with me that she was upset. (Boy, was I wrong.) I didn't know her side of the story, just the story he told me. Her infidelities drove him away from her, and he move back home with his mom. See, I met him while he was living with his mom, and I decided to move him into my place—a complete stranger full of lies and anger problems. He convinced me she was the problem, so I helped him fight against her in court. (I spent hell of money for him to divorce her.) Like always I was just a temporary girlfriend until they could work their differences out. He would cook and clean. We would talk, smoke, and drink together and still fight against his wife. I wanted to carry his baby at some point in time, but thank God that didn't happen. I began to see him as his wife did. He would still be messing around with her until that one fateful day when she called his phone and I picked up. She was so shocked to hear that her husband, the man that could be my father, was dating a young woman like myself. (I was twenty-five, and he was fifty.) We began to talk, and eventually, I released him back to her. He didn't go out with a fight though, and best to believe I was prepared! He had shut my lights off illegally and stole my money. So I took a restraining order out on him and let his job know about his past. Boy, that karma found me again.

He wore his wedding band proudly, never taking it off even when he would meet up with me. He was an officer, and I fell in love with the badge. There is something about a man in uniform that captures my attention. After a week of talking, he ended up in my bed. The way he gazed into my eyes made me literally weak to my knees. What initially was supposed to be just us exchanging numbers so I could clean his house became so much more than that. I knew when he first asked me the question if I cleaned house that was a set up for him to know this new lady at his job. I immediately gave him my number, and I too had my own motive. I knew deep down inside that this wasn't right, but I had an addiction to men with women at home. Anyways, we stop talking and I could tell you more about my tale of being the other woman, but I would rather wait until the next book! I will leave you with this: is the person who is messing with the married person committing adultery although he or she isn't married?

He vowed to love her through it all, but he
just watched her as she began to fall.
Falling from his deceit and lies,
Now he wonders why she sits in the dark and cries!
She vowed to adjust a queen's slipping crown,
but she's the reason the queen frowns!
And I have no doubt in mind that he would be back in my bed again.
He ran through my mind heavily.
How could I be crazy for a man that wasn't even mine, again.

CHAPTER 2

Thy Shall Not Cause No Hurt to Anyone

See, I don't want people to think I've lost the war when I was never trained on the battle. This life that was given to me I was prematurely prepared for it. No one gave me the rules and the warning. So precaution and preparation was nonexistent to me. I wonder about leaving my name engraved in people's hearts and the disbelief of how one could be so cold.

I was just on a search trying to find myself I barely could budge my finances yet along build something with someone. You could say I was opportunistic, but I say I was a person looking for opportunities by any means necessary. My mind didn't process pain well, so I could careless whom I hurt. I met her when I was trying to get established, and we fell instantly. I was twenty, and she was thirty-four, and at thirty-two she still crosses my mind. After all these years I can admit I truly miss the kind-hearted woman that took care of me. Out of all the women that wanted her, she chose me. We got along well, but she had trust issues that would be our downfall. The story went like this:

I was looking for an escape, and she opened her doors to me, allowing a complete stranger to come into her home. She was so possessive, and I was looking for someone who could control me. She was so good to me in the beginning, then everything went left. She assumed everyone liked me at my job, so I quit and tried to go back to school. After one month of school, I quit and went back to work but quit soon after to keep things good between us. Things weren't so good. Her insecurities got the best of her, which caused us to tear apart. I couldn't bear to be falsely accused of things I wasn't doing, and being separated from the world was depressing me. I packed my stuff and moved back to the home I was trying to escape. I called an old friend, and I left her home. That didn't last long because she came back and got me, and like a puppy, I followed her home. Things seem to be getting better, though she let her guard down, and we were more in love with one another than before. She gave me the world, and I gave her pain in the end. One day I woke up and just left again, and this time I disappeared, but when we talk, I could hear all the pain in her voice as she screamed, "You used me and that hurts." I didn't care because she was one more step closer to whatever I was searching for. I wonder about her though, and then again I could care less.

He had adored me since I was sixteen. The first guy who ever wanted to see me smile rather than naked. He would have done anything for me, and I wish I could say the same. I'll never forget that moment when someone stole from me, and he got it back for me. I was so in love with him afterwards because he was that king I wrote about in my fairy tales. That love I had for him would be a short life because of the fast life and the adventures I was seeking. He was like every guy a girl could dream of: polite, charming, respectful, and hardworking. We would communicate through letters and through other people. So many people where in our business, and he allowed that. I was a different type of girl, and the neighborhood guys like that. I was still innocent and reaching high heights to get away from my surroundings. He was so sweet and gullible, and I was carefree and cautious. In my heart he wasn't the one, but I just let the moment play out. He saw nothing but good in me, but I couldn't bear to keep him because he was someone's king not mine! No matter how great he treated me, I couldn't keep him away from his true queen. Over the years we would keep in contact, and he finally found his queen. Although I was an issue in their relationship, he kept fighting to prove that I was irrelevant. We eventually got back together and rekindled the spark we had when we were sixteen. We finally had sex, and he could of kept it but he was convenient. The feelings I used to feel for him was nonexistent, and eventually I hurt him. He said my demanding ways had pushed him to the limit. I was no longer that sweet, innocent girl he once fell for. I had matured and fell into the trap

I once tried to get away from. The difference in me then and now is that I no longer get hurt but causes the hurt.

He took me to places that I ain't never been, surrounded me with things I could only imagine, and showed me things that I was never taught. He was so much older than me, and he was so wise. He thought he could change me, but you can't change a person who doesn't want to be changed. He still tried, so he spoiled me with lavish gifts and money. We would stay up for days and talk about everything. I would be gone for days and come back to him with lies of my whereabouts. Somehow I knew he knew I was lying, but he saw something good in me. My imagination grew wild with him. I use to make up outrageous stories just to con my way out of situations. I would always go back after a long period of time, and he treated me as if I was there the whole time. He never ask questions on where I ran off to, but he was always concerned for my safety though. I knew I was worrying him, but I overlooked that with my selfishness. I would sleep on his couch for days while he slept alone in the bed he bought for us. I never quite understood why this man cared for me the way he did, and not one time did I say thank you!

Finally, his patience run out on me and one crazy night I pulled out of the drive way and I'll never forget the hurt in voice as he yelled my name. He had my favorite wine and made my favorite seafood dinner. The table wasn't barely set, and my first glass of wine was gone already. He asked me with this painful look in his eyes, "Are you going to stay or keep running these streets?" I didn't respond, so he went to the restroom, and when he came back, I had taken the gas money he left for me and the bottles of wine. He yelled my name in pain as I drove out the driveway. He texted my phone. The message read, "You could give a person the world, and they'll still be unappreciative. I've sat back and allowed you to hurt me with your lies. This was your last time, and please don't bring your ass back to my house because you are now unwelcome!"

Like all my other past relations I was just passing through his life. She would kiss me gently as I lay across her bed. I was so tired from the days before that I had finally collapse. When I would open my eyes, there would be food and some sort of gift. She would hold me as I jump from my many nightmares and keep me calm when all hell broke loose.

We balanced each other out, and we were perfectly compatible. I barely had to lift a finger with her, and of course, I didn't have to work either. She would leave me tucked in her covers as she bust her ass at work. I would sneak away sometimes just to get my hands dirty and come back home before she even got off. I was never loyal to her because my mind would always wander. I had the keys to her heart, so she tolerated all my shit. I tore her down daily and watched as she rebuilt herself. She was so strong, and I was weak. How could someone that strong, that kind, and that loyal want someone like me. I would look her dead in her eyes and lie. I would look her dead in her eyes and watch her cry due to the hurt I was causing. She saw through all my bullshit. I was no good for her. Whatever she was looking for, I wasn't it. So one day I pack my stuff and left. She would call and call until one day I got my number changed.

They used to look up to me as if I was doing something great. I was the first to graduate from high school and went on to college. I wanted something different from what I was used to, so I surrounded myself with books and positivity. I worked while in high school just to provide for my family, and I studied hard so I can provide even more for my family. I wanted to pave the way for my siblings, so I pushed my feet on the pedal, but I ended up crashing. I lost it all and had no hopes of gaining it back. I was away from home while they were hurting, hungry, and hopeless. I had traded my college days into party days. (Three times of enrolling in college and I quit all three times.) I made a promise to someone, but I her let down. I became the product of what she feared, but it really didn't matter because she wasn't around. I hurt the people that really looked up to me, but not once did I actually stop and care. I was hurting because I was hurting.

He would leave me flowers of all sorts every morning, and alongside those flowers was a card with a riddle written on it. He would call to make sure I was all right or if had eaten. The admiration he had for me and I had for him was quite visible. Our days were filled of laughter and happiness. We would tell stories underneath the roof of my 2013 Honda Civic. Drinking on the brandy liquor and smoking on a strawberry white owl filled with the best marijuana $35 could buy. I would let him enter my place of warmth but push him off once I climax. We would hold hands until the sweat drip from our palms. He would kiss my forehead before I got into my car and ask when would I be back. I would just smile, saying not a word, and drive off into the middle of the night. I would avoid him because I knew we were just two people having fun until the next moment with someone else. (Well, he thought differently.) He had planned a life for us, and I had found a way to end that plan. One drunken night the lights in his room come on, and there I was with his best friend. The look in his eyes was enough for me to walk away and never come back.

*****

For a moment I forgot where we were. I let temptation take over. Now we were in deep conversation, talking about the overnight sensation, intensified love we just made. What wasn't supposed to happen occurred. Now we looking lost into each other's eyes while our bodies are hungry for more. We were astonished by what just happened, but it was breathtaking at how amazing it was. This night was just for a moment because the morning will arrive, and you will be where you belong and I will be where you left me, clinging on to that moment that wasn't supposed to be.

I'll see you again, but we won't speak. We'll be like two strangers walking by on the sidewalk.

I still think of you and wonder if you're thinking of me, but it wouldn't matter because you belong to someone else. I erased you from my memory but not my heart because that one moment of your time touched my lonely soul.

While you are near her, I'll be here wishing I was her and clinching my sheets, crying in the spot where you made me feel a temporary love that lasted only an hour and forty-five minutes.

I close my eyes and count to ten.

Opened my eyes to readjust myself.

Clearing my thoughts of you, my dear.

Because I'll be a fool to assume you'll ever want me!

But I must admit that moment that wasn't supposed to happen was the best loving I've had since then!

But then again,

I closed my eyes and here we are again, you in my arms for this temporary moment.

She loves through hurt!
Stabbing herself until she feels no pain,
She buries her feelings deep into the dirt,
While she tries to cleanse her soul with the morning rain.
Eyes full of blackness,
Tongue swollen from lies,
Heart torn of sadness,
Silent cries,
She hurts because she's hurting!

CHAPTER 3

Thy Shall Not Lie, Steal, or Kill

I was brought up to tell the truth no matter what. Truth defines a person's character and is the gateway to a peaceful conscience. Thou shall not lie unless the truth is too hard to tell. Have you ever got a bump on your tongue after telling a big lie? Or in the middle of a lie, have you ever bitten your tongue? Below are the lies that I had to keep going with!

*****

Tickle me silly, full of jokes to you, my dear. I was unfaithful and untrue. Those used condoms you found all hidden in the trash outside your house was indeed mine. In your house and all on your bed, I got head from your ex-best friend. I told you I was sleeping, that's why I didn't answer your call, when the truth was I was creeping with your next-door neighbor. Lies on top of lies, I could've cared less about your silly cries. Throughout our relationship, 90 percent of the times I cheated was because I became bored. I can't say I'm sorry for the lies I told because if I had to do it all over again I would probably still lie to you.

Tickle me silly, full of laughs, oh my love. I created many unfaithful and untrue moments. To you, I was lying to get what and where I needed to be. I created a life that I had never lived just so you could feel sad and blue. She wasn't my best friend, but the girl I loved instead. I moved her in, so when you were gone, us girls would have a little fun. When you caught us in the act, I wasn't worried because I had a lie to tell.

Filled you up with possibilities of me being the one. Lured you into my web of lies, then I sucked you dry, leaving you without life. I wasn't who you thought I was, and neither were you, so I had to lie to keep you onboard. I wasn't too busy to make time for you; I was just occupied with someone new. You were a second choice, just in case I got bored of him. When you would ask questions, I would lie to you, of course. What sense would it make to tell you the truth?

Growing up as a child, stealing was not tolerated. If you couldn't afford, it wasn't meant for you to have it. As I grew up, stealing was so much more than taking something that didn't belong to you physically. Most people don't understand that you can steal the joy out of a person, steal their energy and any aspirations they have.

I met you in the midst of my dark days, you were that light that lit the blackness in my heart. You gave me so much and showed me that this world had much more to offer than frowns and hate. You had so much joy that I couldn't do nothing but envy you. I wondered how you could be this happy when the world gave you nothing but a pile of shit. You saw the good in everything and everyone, a heart full of *godly* joy! I wanted you to see the world for what it really was, so I tore you down, stealing every piece of joy you could ever have. Years later you found that joy I once stole.

I've never met a person whose energy was so positive and powerful as yours. You didn't let your circumstances stop you from conquering what was meant for you until you met me. I created disasters that would drain your energy, leaving you on a negative charge. I made you view the world as I did, nothing but negativity. So you would overdose on misery, and I would be right there with you. Weeks after we departed that dark cloud I brought cleared over from your life, and you found that positive energy that I had stolen.

The center of attention, the main attraction, and beautiful as ever, you had it all. You had money, family, friends, a career, and aspirations. You tried to inspire me to do better than what I was doing, but I wasn't trying to hear that. You invited me around your colleagues, and I gave them my ass to kiss. You even took a chance and gave a job that I made you lose. You almost achieved your lifetime dream, but I stole that dream out through my envious ways. Months later you created something better and rebuilt the aspiration that I once stole from you.

You were in your sad days of your life, and I sensed your vulnerability. I took advantage of your weakness and conned my way into you lonely heart. I needed a place to rest, and you gave me a bed. I brought nothing but more pain to you. I have one motive: to get what I can. So I stole some cash and the bed you supplied me. Off into the night, the thief I was. Now you are more cautious of women like me.

Thou shall not kill the person who carries a soul full of guilt, hurt, lies, truth, and motives. Like stealing, a person call kill you without causing bodily injury. The intention of killing a person: a sickening desire of a person who is lacking something in their life so they kill and steal the life from another person.

All you wanted from me was nothing but the truth! I couldn't give you that, so each day we were together I killed you slowly with my actions. So in love with me you stayed around, and I watched you die figuratively as I continuously committed my unfaithfulness ways.

You wanted nothing but the best for me even though I didn't. You gave me the tools and prepared me properly. I had it all and lost control. It was you who tried to bring me back down. I killed you instantly when I said, "Fuck you, I don't need you anymore."

You loved me regardless of my past, and you saw nothing but the goodness in me. I was on the road to recovery, but from time to time I would relapse. I know you didn't understand although you said you did, but I wouldn't expect you to, when your path was paved clean and clear for you. You thought you could handle my quick temper and bad attitude, but I was way past a level you could ever handle. This time out of my life someone walked away from me, and it killed you to see me weeks later on to the next person.

Dear God, I am everything my mom feared me to be.
I've murdered people with my lies.
I've stolen from so many people.
I've lied just to lie, and I've continuously done so.

CHAPTER 4

Thy Should Love Myself

I didn't know how to love myself, so therefore I deprived myself from being loved by some people who actually meant good to me. I had kept a list of every man and woman I had ever been with. I did this because I wanted to remember the countless moments I lay down with these people. A few were relationships, one-night stands, wasn't suppose too happen, and eventually bound to happen. Reading through the names I could tell you exactly where I was in that moment in life.

Dear Self,

Mirror, mirror on the floor cracked into a million pieces, did I really deserve to have my head slammed into you? Looking at myself through the shattered glass covered in red and scattered across the floor, I thought, *Damn, not again*. How did I let things escalate? When I say thing escalate, I mean we were just having a heated discussion on missing money and his lack of contribution. How did I let it get this way? When I say this way, I mean I allowed this man to use my face and my body as his own private punching bag. Every time we have a disagreement, this happens. I know I should go, but my feet won't let me walk. It was as if my heart was sending my feet a message saying, "Don't you walk out on love. Besides, girl, you know he loves you and you know it want happen again!" Mirror, mirror cracked into a million pieces, boy, was my heart wrong!

Faces became names, and names became numbers. Eventually I began to lose track of those numbers, and all those numbers became memories. Those fading memories became dark shadows of my past. Dark shadows of men and women who used to lust and love all over my body. To be loved is what I wanted, so I searched for love in all ways possible. I would tolerate anything just to be loved. Different men and women in and out my life, and I never committed even though I wanted to. I got lost within my search, and when love was shown to me, I became blind to the affection. Physical, mental, and emotional, I allowed myself to be abused because that was what I thought love was.

My head hung low, and my heart was beaten and abused. If this was the love I wish for, I wish this wish undone quickly. Beauty became my beast, and shame became my life. My skin had become a permanent mark that even the darkness couldn't hide the bruises. I was supposed to love and cherish my life, but how could I love when it was never shown to me. If this how love is, I'd rather take a knife across my own throat, but then again my heart does deserve a second chance. I stayed in so many situations knowing I should leave, but where could I go when I had no place to go? If love meant crying all day and afraid to fall asleep, I would have thought about it before I went searching for it.

He used me because I allowed him to, draining me all that I had, and still he didn't love me. I crept around with him, hiding in the shadows so his wife wouldn't know, and he still stayed with her. He fed my head with a bunch of lies, and I fell for every single one, and he still didn't love me. Got him to where he needed to be and he switched up on me. He would only call me for sexual favors, and I would go running to him, but that still didn't make him love me. I would kiss the ground he walked on, and nope, that still didn't make him love me.

*****

Self-love is so important!
If you know how to love yourself, then others will too.
Self-love is amazing!
There are so many young girls, ladies, and women out here who have walked or is walking in my shoes right now who need to know that love is not pain.
Love is beautiful!
So find someone who loves you as much as you love you!
Thy shall love myself!

CHAPTER 5

Thy Shall Not Keep
Quiet nor be Afraid!

Thy shall not keep quiet to protect the person who is causing harm.
Closed mouths can cause much more serious hurt to someone in the
future. I kept my mouth shut nice and tight because I was afraid to upset
the ones around me. My erotic behavior and failure to commit is due to
the abuse I locked tightly in my mind.

I would lock myself in my room hoping soon they would dismiss
themselves. Friends of my relative, they would watch me with temptation
in their eyes and make inappropriate comments.

I was only but a child, all pure and innocent to the world. I stood
out from the rest, when in reality all I wanted to do in blend in with the
rest. Discomfort from the stares, I covered myself until they would pass.

Dear Mama,

I never told you, but it's true. It weighs on me heavily.
Only but eight, he took advantage. Touch me roughly
until I press the gas, then instantly he released me fast.
(Went for a ride with a family friend) Felt all dirty, so
I washed real good. Kept quiet 'cause I was ashamed.
Secret with me until I was ready to spill the beans on
what he did. Shock to my eyes, he no longer exists. I
erased him in my head. I did indeed. That one eager
ride alone changed my life, for now I have the courage

to speak. Thy shall not keep quiet even if I'm afraid because someone else is going through the same thing.

To my friend of many years,

You knew it was going to happen, but you said nothing to me. All quiet and plotting, you left me with them. Three of them all in my face, they knew I was all drunk and out. Scared out my mind, so I played along as they tugged on me and tickled me with jokes. Friend, how could you leave me all down in blue? Three guys in my face staring at me. Heart beating out my chest right then and there, I was so afraid. Two left me, and there was one. He undressed me, but I was too weak to fight. On top of me with dirty socks that smell, I prayed that the penetrating would be over soon. All I could do to fight him is yell and scream for him to stop. Then I thought of you, my friend, and remembered what you told me before. Closed my eyes and counted to ten, and then he was done and gone. Cleaned myself and took a deep breath. When the morning come, it'll all be okay. Said not a word because I was afraid that my life would be taken.

To you,

My kin, how could you laugh at me when I told you the truth, so help me God! He sent a picture of himself all exposed from the neck all down. I was uncomfortable, but you always tried to get me to work with him. If only you know what I would have to do then, that smirk you carry would no longer exist. Word around town he did this before, but you think everyone is lying. Because he's you kin, it can't be true. He was a predator that preyed on women but, like you, only in the dark. One late night I received a message. I opened that message. It was from him all exposed and comparing himself with the hand remote control all comfortably placed. Then just like that it disappeared, but you wouldn't believed me, so I kept quiet and carried that secret, for I put it in my mind all tightly stored because I was afraid I would be an outcast.

To that guy I met at the hotel while we both were working,

It wasn't until a year later we linked up, and I could tell you adored me, but you had a girlfriend. We would talk and laugh for hours as if tomorrow didn't matter. I was so comfortable around you that I didn't care about anything. I wanted to just have sex with you while you wanted a deeper connection with me. You saw a wife in me, but I only saw a friend in you. We would disappear from each other, well, I would disappear from you and then come back as if I hadn't gone anywhere. You would tell me jokes to keep my spirits up and encouraged me when I had self-doubts. You were so perfect to me even with your flaws, but I wasn't ready to be anyone's everything. Here we are, a year or two later, and you, my friend, still see the hidden beauty within me. Our conversation is so intense now that my smile is indeed pure and full of love for you. Although I missed my moment with you, that next person will be one lucky woman. (I kept quiet on how I felt about you.)

Open your mouth and speak your fear
Let it be heard loud and clear.
Do not be afraid because the truth
Isn't always pretty.
Fear is a clutch, holding you back,
So don't be afraid to take that risk.

CHAPTER 6

Thy Shall Forgive and Forget

I was always told too forgive others even if it hurts you. I was always told you would never heal if you never address the issue and move past it. Forgiveness shows that you have power and that you understand that people make bad choices. I was always told that God forgives me for my choices, so I should forgive others. I was told that to fully forgive someone you also have to forget! Well, I'll never forget, just in case that person does the same thing again.

Dear Daddy,

There are so many things I could say negatively right now, but I would rather store the pain and anger I have in the Lord's hands. I can't bear to carry this load of your selfishness, your inconsiderateness, the poor excuse of a father anymore, so I pray not only for me but for you as well. I could say I *hate*, but instead I'm saying *I love you*! You taught me one of the most valuable lessons a father could teach their daughter. That lesson is to not rely on anyone, especially your father. You gave me something that I carried throughout my life—the will to do it on my own and being strong. See, when you weren't around, I fought through it all. I carried the load while my mother was alive, when she passed away, and until now. Not once have you apologized for missing out on our lives or for not being able to protect us from harm—molestation, abuse, self-hatred, and suicide. Not once have you tried to amend the relationship with your daughters, only your favorite. What about me though or your other daughter and grandkids? You weren't a father to your daughters, but there's still a chance to step up and be a grandfather. You painted this picture to everyone that you are a good person. You're as worse than the man who put his hands on me. I could go deeper into the inappropriate touching when I was only eight years old and I could talk about the sexual assaults and verbal assaults, but I'd rather not. God is dealing with those men. I pray he has mercy on you. I've tried constantly to build with you, and constantly you failed me. You rather chase whores than chase your daughters. You rather support another man's daughter when you have never, ever supported or went out of your way for your daughters. Yes, you allowed us to stay with you, but we paid rent, although you have never taken care of us and you were behind on child support. Everything you ever gave us was still yours even though you *gave* it to us as a gift. You called us stupid because of the people we deal with. I wondered what made my mom marry you. (Was she stupid?) Growing up, I remember the times when it did feel like you were a father. You showed us off like we were trophies. Trophies you stole from someone else because you damn sure didn't deserve us. You always said my mom withheld information, basically making you look bad, but as I grew up, I saw that the information was actually accurate.

On the outside it looks like I'm well put together, but on the inside I'm a freaking mess. A ball of fire that burns because I lost one parent and the other parent never showed any affection. No *congratulations, great job, well done, next time you'll be better, love you, are you okay, you deserve better, never anger* when some man has verbally, mentally, and physically abused your daughter. (Always has that dumb smirk and look on your face!) Growing up, my sisters were picked on by men. I stood up for them, but who stood up for me?

Dear you,

Beaten until my breath was gone, then you put life back into me with your own breath. Fought so hard, my hands carried bruises of new and old. Body marked up with healed and fresh new wounds, you would think I was a graffiti board. Swollen eyes from all the crying I did and busted lip from you putting me in my place. We fought so much until the point when the dogs went to hide when they heard the glass shatter across the room. You took me for the trash the world disposed me to be, but I never exposed myself to be treated like trash! From sleeping on the cold porch when you would put me out to sleeping in your bed when the cash flow was right. I was your lady with a heart to give you a beat. Bloodstains on the white shirt you wore as I rode in the ambulance, saying, "I'm done." You taught me a valuable lesson about life—that it's better to go than to stay with hell. I forgave the pain you caused but won't forget the storm I walked through with you!

Dear sister,

May you find peace in the pit of your soul.
May you find forgiveness in the center of your heart.
May you find love within your blood flow.
May you find happiness within the mirror soon.
Dear sister of mine, may your blessing overflow.
May your prayers be heard loud and clear.
May you find strength within the Lord.
May you find courage through your fears.
May your life be filled of prosperous moments.
May you rest easy at night
And find comfort in the day.
For you, my sister of the same parents, may you find
what you are looking for as I have been shut out from
your life.

I forgive you, but I'll never forget.
Understand that I'm not weak because I accepted what you did.
I only forgave you because karma is a bitch and
you'll receive exactly what you gave to me.

CHAPTER 7

Thy Shall Learn to Heal

They say to move on from a bad situation you must be healed. Mental, physically, spiritually and emotionally healed. A healthy mind and heart is a healed mind and heart.

I kept quiet about my struggles! I didn't want anyone to know about what I was dealing with. They spoke of people who were like me, and it was far from positive. They would think I was crazy and leave me in my own sad thoughts. They wouldn't offer help or even an ear to listen, so I said nothing and fought this battle alone. For a minute I even wondered if God was real, hell, if he even existed. It was eating me up inside. I hate the day and feared the night. Find a hobby, they say, but what good is a hobby when you have no interest, no motivation, and no strength. I literally felt like I was dying every day I got out of bed. I wanted to reach out for help, but what's help when you can't even help yourself. I would sit in my car, smoking and drinking, wishing I was somewhere else. I didn't like myself, and I always lived in the past, of the good days I did remember. I try to heal, but I don't know how. Man, depression is real, and I'm just trying find ways to heal from it.

Gun in my hand, thinking of shooting myself in my heart that hurts or my head that's filled with unprocessed thoughts. I sit in this car, windows rolled up, drink in my cup, while I'm contemplating on swallowing this whole bottle of pills. I cannot swim, nor can I float. I sit at the edge of that wooden dock. Feet dangling as I stare off into space, thinking of the loves that I'll leave behind. Cars racing down this dark road, with no sign of light anywhere, so I'll dress in all black and jump out without even thinking about it. Soak in the hot bath tub of misery, candles burning alongside of the brand-new razor I just bought. The right vein will ease the pain as I fade into whatever comes after death. I'll probably wished that somehow I would be healed from these suicidal thoughts I have.

These scars will heal, they say, but what about the ugly marks they leave. I'm constantly reminded of what almost damaged me. The doctors said I wasn't going to make it, so my mom prayed that God would make a miracle happen. Down syndrome, they assumed I would have, and a life of struggle I would face. I was only a fetus, and I had already be labeled. Day and night on her knees she prayed for a baby who would be all healthy and strong. I had a knot blocking my air passage in the womb, so I wasn't getting oxygen to my brain. A doctor mystery, they could not wait for the fetus to come out. I was born and immediately taken into surgery, and from that day on I had multiple surgeries. That mysterious lump would be removed but appeared again only in a different spot. I was so embarrassed because my wrist are different sides, and you can see the ugly marks. They say the scars will heal, but what about the girl who carried around the shame of being different from the rest.

I could not lie nor could I hide. I cried and cried until I became what I feared. They called me names in my face as well as behind my back. I was not like the popular kids, so I became an easy target. I was laughed at and bullied to the point I hated my flawless brown skin. I didn't see beauty in my eyes, so I walked in the shadows of someone else. I laughed, and I pointed. I became the bully I once indeed feared. I knew better, and there is no excuse for my behavior. I do am truly sorry for the people who felt my pain. I am not healed from my past, and I regret for the people who suffered under my reign.

They laughed as I walked past, hoping I would trip over my own feet. They stared at me while whispering lies that they created in their own little mind. They broke me with every remark they made, and I allowed them. I would go home and stare in the mirror and say, "Why?" I was an outcast because I was different, so they excluded me from everything, and the reason why was because I was always too busy. They would pray for my downfall, while I prayed for them to come up.

I would watch them eat while my stomach aches for just a little crumb. I would go without before I would ever ask them because I didn't want my business all in the streets. I tried to trust, and I tried to heal, but sometimes it harder than said.

Dear Lord, heal me from what has weakened me.

CHAPTER 8

Thy Shall Cherish Every Moment of Life

The best things in life are made to be a memorable event. When I was down and out, I used to think of the moments I cherished.

We shared the same laughter and tears. I remember we were the best of friends, always walking in each other's shadow. I admire y'all, and y'all admired me. It was us against the world, and we defended our world to the maximum. Playing house and school, creating messes in the closet in our room, we shared giggles while telling stories under the table tent we built. We were inseparable—the three blind mice, the three little bears, and mamas three little angels. Oh my, how I miss those times when we sat at the table together and ate or how we sat on the couch and watched our favorite Disney movie. Times like that I wish I could relive and relive over and over again.

Wooden chairs with square cushions all covered in flowers, television missing a knob so we used pliers, and fans in the windows to keep us cool. Playing in the living room while laughing at the corny jokes the drunken uncles used to tell and listening to the oldies. Sweet smell of Sunday dinner blessed the house as we arrive from church. Grandma's hands all covered in food because she was preparing a feast for her family and friends. The sound of laughter carried from the house to the outside, you would think we were having a party. Family and friends sat at the table, giving thanks for Grandma's hands.

Whistling and whiskey on hand, he sat on the porch, waving his hands to passing cars, tapping his feet while patting his leg to the rhythm of the beat of the song playing on his record player. Playing horseshoe with the nearby neighbors, laughing and joking. How I missed that view! Sitting on the steps as I arrived from school, making sure I made it home safely. Scolding and loving, manners and discipline he taught while still being that grumpy old grandpa. Honest and brutal, broken and beaten man, that old man had stories for days. Some was real, and let's just say some was fabricated, but to have a moment where Granddaddy would be here to tell another crazy story would be amazing.

Dairy Queen, every time you saw us was the most memorable moment we had with you. From taking rides to just leaving us and not knowing when you'll come back, you were always a mystery and deep, dark one at that. Blocking out the bad moments you showed us—well, at least I did because I saw good in you. You messed up so much that I'm asking how could I have forgiven you. That moment you spent at Dairy Queen overpowered the craziness you had in you. The rides on your motorcycle and the scar it left as my leg got burned was worth the pain because who knew of the next time I would see you. Now I'm older and I have a voice, but apparently your ears cannot hear the pain you caused. So I relive that time you took me to Dairy Queen.

When the world seem all messed up, you were there to help me arrange things. When I was sick and contagious, you were there, ready to be my doctor. When I needed a friend, you were there and never left. Fed me when I was hungry, clothed me, and cleaned me, a superhero you were. You were head of the family, and strong you were until life had beaten you down. I have never seen you cry until that day you had to say good-bye. There was a lost look in your eyes, knowing that when the sun rises you would no longer be around. You gave me such great memories that it's hard to even remember the bad memories. From wiping my tears to holding me close, those morning hugs and good night kisses I'll always remember for I miss them so much.

I closed my eyes, and there you were, a pretty little thing who would be my boo. You gave me joy and purpose to live. Although you weren't mine, you gave me a new meaning in life. You looked up to me, and I could tell this by the way you smiled as I embraced you in my arms. I felt like my life had a meaning with you, so when you were around I kept it positive, for I didn't want you to know the struggles I was dealing with.

Thank you for giving me the definition of what love is again because you saw through all my flaws.

If no one loved me, you showed me you did. So sweet and pure, what a joy you are to my life. Quiet and shy, you gave me laughter with you corny little jokes. Although you weren't mine, you gave my heart a joyful beat to follow. I could tell you love me by the way you smiled at me. All happy inside I gave you joy. We would dance and talk, play and laugh. You were that little boy who saved me from drowning in my own misery. Thank you for seeing the good in me through all my imperfections.

So tiny and rough but yet a lovable teddy bear, you are a breath of freedom in my confined life. We would stay up all hour of the night, playing, talking, and laughing. You would surprise me as I walked in the house from a long day's work, and then we would began our night of fun. I would try to make you go to bed, but you would wait until I fell asleep. My protector and angel from this dangerous road I walk. You gave me a reason to be more cautious, and that was why I came home every night just to see you try to scare me. Thank you for being my shield from all the danger that I faced every day.

Enemies and friends we are! Our relationship is unexplainable. Just know we love one another no matter where this road take us. Though distance and arguments divide us, our love was so strong that we always found our way back together. You were one of the first friends I ever made that gave me that push to stay. I had my self-doubts, but you were there to takes those doubts and trash them. Same struggles but different paths. Deep down inside I always looked up to you. From fights to love to now we are here understanding one another so we can grow and catch up on the years we missed because of our stubbornness. Thank you for always believing in me even when I fell.

Change is inevitable.
Make memories.
Enjoy the time.
Love them now.
Cherish each day because tomorrow isn't promised!

CHAPTER 9

Thy Shall Apologize for
All My Wrongdoings!

I was always told that apologies comes from a place where the words "I'm sorry" or "I apologize" come from.

I admit I'm not perfect; and I've broken a lot of hearts, homes, and friendships. I've come to the point in life where I am ashamed of what I did and how I acted. If I could redo this life, I would jump to it quick, fast, and in a hurry to do so. There is so many things I could have thought long and hard about and so many opportunities I would have taken. Maybe then a lot of things in my life would have turned out differently. Well, I can't live in the past. All I can do is make the future right by apologizing and moving on. I have uncovered my sins and acknowledged them. Please forgive me!

Although I have never apologized face-to-face with these women and never met some of them, my apologies. I apologize to the women who thought their husbands were happy but yet were lusting and loving over my body. I should have stayed away from the temptation and the gifts that were thrown my way. I never asked about you nor did I care about you, but I wondered if you knew your king was being deceitful. That never stopped me from meeting up with them from time to time though. I could only imagine if the shoe were on the other foot. How would I feel? I ask for forgiveness, for I have broken one of the Ten Commandments: "Thy shall not commit adultery!"

To the many people I let down on multiple occasions, I do apologize. When I was in the darkest places of my life, you never gave up on me.

You continue to believe in me even when I disappointed you. There were so many people who saw so much in me even when I saw little in myself. They gave me opportunities that I failed to complete. I had given up on myself because it was what I was used to. I became weary in doing good, so at the proper time, I didn't reap a harvest because I gave up.

To the many people who followed me, I apologize for leading you down the wrong path and leaving you. I was so lost. How could someone like me help anyone find their path? I walked down this dark road without a light, so I was completely in blackness, blind to life due to my own fears and defeated by my own failures. I walk through the valley of the shadow of death, and I did fear evil, for I felt God wasn't with me and the rod and staff were not there to comfort me.

To the many men that saw a wife in me even when I was never into it, I apologize for holding you up from your true wife. See, you saw something in me that I wasn't ready to reveal nor willing to reveal. I was so into the things that didn't really matter that I forgot what really did matter. I emotionally drained you with all my childish ways, and I physically tired you out with all the chasing you had to do. I hope wherever you are now that she is treating you right and giving you the love and respect you deserve. You thought you had found a good thing, but your perception was wrong.

I apologize to myself for allowing myself to fall deeper into this dark place and not seek help because I was ashamed. I was ashamed for allowing these men to take advantage of me and mislead me during my most vulnerable times and for thinking that I could find happiness in the arms of someone else's man and for bringing chaos to the relationship. I apologize to myself for not being woman enough or confident enough to admit I was wrong. I am sorry for all the false promises I made and the fake dreams I sold, for my failures and my unaccomplished dreams. There were so many days when my greed overpowered my generosity and my negative thoughts overpowered the positive thoughts. I know I've done wrong and made a lot of mistakes, but he that has not sin should cast the first stone at me. If you have not done anything wrong in life, don't be so quick to judge anyone.

Everyone's story is different, and not everyone will agree with your story. The funny thing about life is that people are quick to judge by the cover of the book and they haven't even opened the damn book up. They look at the outside of the book and automatically come up with a summarized version. Life is different for everyone, and everyone handles it differently. We were born as a blank canvas, and we painted our own picture with the paintbrush we were blessed with.

The End

CPSIA information can be obtained
at www.ICGtesting.com
Printed in the USA
LVHW112048020320
648718LV00007B/1054